The Candy Coated Castle's

Catastrophe

A Christmas Crisis

'A critical thinking reader"

D1506505

Francis Patrick Theriault

Outskirts Press, Inc.
Denver, Colorado

The Candy Coated Castle's Catastrophe
A Christmas Crisis

Illustrated by
Stacy Mitchell

Outskirts Press
http://www.outskirtspress.com

ISBN-10: 1-59800-555-3
ISBN-13: 978-1-59800-555-4

Outskirts Press and the "OP" logo are trademarks belonging to Outskirts Press, Inc.

Printed in the United States of America

Vocabulary & Spelling Words

These should be given to students before they read the appropriate Chapter(s).

CHAPTERS 1 & 2

crisis flustered disappointed murmured depressed
rectangular squinting
cackled scribbled

CHAPTER 3

splendidly bargain doubtful contract frightful plucked
hideous hovering twirled

CHAPTERS 4 & 5

funk twinkled snickered tournament bragging blustered

CHAPTER 6

advanced creatures loophole refreshed conclusion
original document
commoner solve

CHAPTERS 7 & 8

munching approached perspiration considering temptation
faith   charms
Twirled jiggled indicate ignored flourished leered
hideous

CHAPTERS 9 & 10

representing sputtered lunged asphalt casually awesome
recount
stuffed   disagreeing

The teacher may decide to add to this list or subtract those words deemed inappropriate. (Another good word!)

Group Questions for Discussion

These questions are meant to help students discuss the story. Teachers should be free to follow up with other questions which may generate critical thinking.

CHAPTERS 1-2

1. Why do you think Page likes Princess?

2. Why is Charlie Chocolate Drop so important to Candiesville?

3. Who do you think Sammy Satin really is?

4. Why do you think the twins laughed when Sweetooth said, "Will that do?"

CHAPTER 3

1. Why do you think Satin did not give Sweetooth a copy of the contract immediately?

2. What can Sweetooth do about his problem? Explain.

3. What do you think the Ladies-in-waiting are supposed to do for Queen Bob Bon?

4. Do they seem to do a good job? Explain.

CHAPTERS 4-5

1. Why would Queen Bon Bon select Blue Dolphin for a snack?

2. Describe agent Double Double O O.

3. What do you think he can do to help Sweetooth?

CHAPTER 6

1. Is Agent very smart? Why do you think so?

2. Was Agent's father's advice, "always do your best" good advice? Explain.

3. Explain why Sweetooth doesn't think Page is good enough for Princess.
4. Do you think he is correct? Why?

CHAPTERS 7-8

1. Who is Desiree?

2. What made Satin accept Desiree's challenge? Is this sensible? Why or why not?

CHAPTERS 9-10

1. Why was everyone concerned about the twins being allowed to referee?

2. Why didn't they have to worry?

3. Do you think Sweetooth will change his mind about Page? Why or why not?

These questions are meant to help students discuss the story. Teachers should be free to follow up with other questions which may generate critical thinking.

CHAPTER 1

THE CHOCOLATE COVERED PEANUT

Once upon a time, in the tiny kingdom of Candiesville, just as Christmas was approaching, a terrible crisis happened.

King Sweetooth and Queen Bon Bon were sitting on their thrones eating some chocolate covered peanuts with their daughter, Princess Candy Cane, when the Princess swallowed one of the candies whole and began to choke. The Queen, who was quite athletic, jumped from her throne and slapped her daughter on the back. The candy popped out of her mouth, like a rocket shot from Mars, and hit the King's nose.

"Ow," he cried. "You didn't have to do that, Princess."

"She couldn't help it, Sweetie," the Queen said softly. "Besides, she's all better now and your nose

has just a little bump on it."

Sweetooth rubbed his nose.

"No one will ever notice it," the Queen declared. "now where did that candy go?"

Just then, Page rushed into the room yelling, "King Sweetooth! King Sweetooth! We are in trouble!" Before he could say anything else, his body flipped up in the air and came down right in front of Princess Candy Cane.

She placed her hand on his face and cried, "Oh, Page, are you all right?"

Page blushed. "I am now."

Queen Bon Bon came to remove her daughter's hand from the Page's face. "What happened, Page?"

"He slipped on that stupid candy peanut," Sweetooth shouted, bending over to take a better look at Page.

"What happened to your nose?" Page asked.

The Queen thought that was funny and laughed. So did the Princess.

Sweetooth didn't laugh. He became flustered, put his hand over his face, and asked Page, "Why are we in trouble?"

Page sat up. "It's Charlie! Charlie Chocolate! Charlie Chocolate Drop!"

"What about old Charlie?" Sweetooth asked.

"He done dropped!"

"Charlie Chocolate Drop dropped?"

"Yes, sire. They took him to Peppermint Memorial Hospital in the Candy Wagon. No one at the Candy Factory knows what to do without Charlie. They all went home."

Sweetooth helped Page to his feet. "Are you all right now?"

"Yes, sire. What should I do?"

"You go home and rest for now. I'll think of something."

Page started to leave, turned around and smiled at the Princess, who smiled back."

She held out the bag of chocolate covered peanuts. "Would you like one?"

"No, thanks," Page said. "I've had one already." He left the room much happier than when he came in.

Queen Bon Bon was upset. "This is our busiest time of the year. How will we get all the Christmas orders out? No one can take Charlie Chocolate Drops place. No one."

"And what about all the children who look forward to Santa bringing them candy for Christmas? He gets all of his sweets from us. They'll be so disappointed, Daddy."

Sweetooth looked at them both and tried to put on a brave face. "There, there," he murmured. "Why don't you both have a nice swim in the Royal Pool."

"I can't swim, Daddy. You know that."

"Sit on your mother, then. She can lie on her back and float for hours."

"Can I sit on you, Mother? Like Daddy said? Can I?"

"May I. May I sit on your stomach," her mother said.

"But you're bigger than me," Princess Candy Cane wailed.

"I meant you don't ask permission by using the word can. Can means are you able. You say may. May I?"

"All right, Mother. May I?"

"As long as you don't jump up and down like you did last time, dear," Queen Bon Bon replied as they left the King sitting on his throne looking very sad.

WHAT WILL HAPPEN

TO SAVE THE KING AND

CANDIESVILLE? WHY?

CHAPTER 2

SWEETOOTH SOLVES HIS PROBLEM.
OR, DOES HE?

King Sweetooth sat on his throne the rest of the day and all through the night, thinking and thinking and thinking. "What can I do?" he cried out in the empty room. Nobody answered.

It began raining outside and the King became more depressed. By morning he was still on the throne, slumped over like a person who was sick to his stomach. Once again he cried out in frustration, "What can I do? What can I do?"

The rain stopped and the sun shone brightly through one of the oversized rectangular windows, reaching out and finding Sweetooth's face. He covered his eyes and groaned.

"I can help you, sire," a deep voice spoke from the doorway.

The King straightened up. "What?"

The voice spoke again. "I can help you solve your problem, sire. With the candy."

Sweetooth stood, squinting his eyes. "Where the blazes are you, then?"

"Right here, sire." And so he was. A skinny faced man, dressed in red and black, stood before Sweetooth. He smiled showing yellow teeth. Standing behind him were two other men. One was short and pudgy. The other was short and pudgy. They were, in fact, twins, wearing identical red hats, shirts, pants and shoes. They even had little red rimmed glasses which hid their red lined eyes.

"What happened to your nose," the leader asked.

"Yes," the twins spoke as one voice. "It looks comical."

Sweetooth turned around, hoping to see Bon Bon so he could say, "See? Everyone does notice it." But she was not there. She was still in bed.

"It's not my nose that's the problem," Sweetooth replied.

"I know that," the leader smiled as the twins cackled in stereo. "You need help at the factory. Getting the Christmas orders out." He leaned toward Sweetooth, his breath smelling of garlic. "Isn't that correct?"

The King wiggled is nose and sat down. He was tired. "Yes, it is the problem. And who are you? And how can you fix it?"

"My name is Sammy Satin, the greatest candy factory foreman in the universe. The twins are my personal assistants. Danny and Billy Devilton. The greatest candy factory workers in the universe. You, sire, are in luck."

Sweetooth yawned and tried to sit up straight. "Why would you help me, Mr. Satin? I don't know you."

"Because, sire, you are going to help me." Sammy pulled a paper from his back pocket and produced a pen.

"Just sign on the dotted line and everything is going to be just fine."

The King yawned three more times before he took the pen and scribbled his signature on the document. "Will that do?"

Sammy and the twins gazed at the paper and laughed so hard they cried.

The twins turned at the door to ask Sweetooth in one frightfully grating voice, "Will that *do*?"

This question struck them so funny they slammed into each other and fell to the floor before finally leaving the room.

Sweetooth fell asleep thinking the crisis was now behind him. He slept all day and all night.

SWEETOOTH PEEKING OUT FROM BENEATH THE COVERS AT QUEEN BON BON

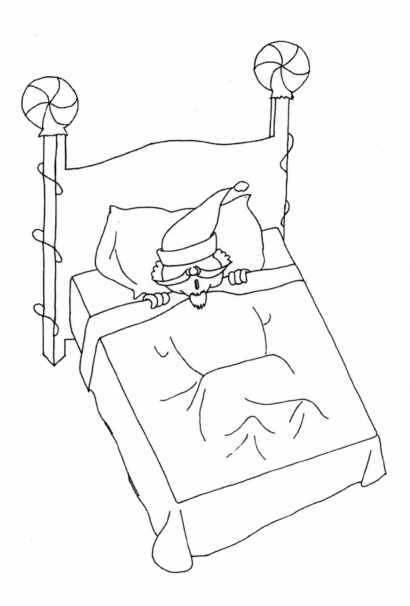

CHAPTER 3
A SUNNY DAY TURNS GLOOMY

A t daybreak, the sun rose to shine splendidly on King Sweetooth, sleeping soundly under the quilted covers of his king sized bed.

Queen Bon Bon rushed into the room and leapt upon the bed to wake him up. She landed, accidentally, on his left leg. "Sorry, Sweetie," she whispered.

The King threw back the covers and made a face. "First my nose. Now my leg. Am I such an easy target? And why are you waking me at this hour?'

"This hour?" She laughed loudly. "My dear, it is almost noon. You can't hide under those covers all day."

"Why not? I'm the king, aren't I?"

"Of course you are. Which means you have kingly things to do. So get up and do them."

"What kind of kingly things?"

"The factory is running at full speed. The men you hired are awesome!"

"Men? What men?"

"That Sammy character and those fat little twins."

Sweetooth sat straight up in bed. "By jove, I do remember those three." He smiled. "Are they really that good?"

"Better than Charlie."

"Nonsense! Nobody's better than Charlie."

"Charlie is in the hospital. And they have the Candy Factory humming."

"That's a relief."

"How much did you have to pay them," Queen Bon Bon asked, fear creeping into her face.

'That's the best part! Nothing!"

"Nothing?"

"Nothing. All I did was sign a stupid scrap of paper." He stood up and waved his hand in the air.

"That sounds too good to be true."

"They wanted more, but I drove a hard bargain."

"You drove a hard bargain?" She looked doubtful. "Where is the paper?"

"They took it."

"You didn't get a copy?"

"I was sleepy. I'm sure that Sammy fellow will bring me one."

And at that very moment, he did! Sammy strolled through the bedroom door as if he owned the place.

"I say, old chap. This is my private bedroom." Sweetooth said.

"Right now, maybe. But not for long." Sammy wiggled his nose.

Sweetooth rubbed his. "What do you mean by that statement?"

Sammy drew a piece of paper from his back pocket. "This is a copy of what you signed, oh great and mighty king. It would be wise to read it." He handed the paper to Sweetooth. "Wiser to have read it yesterday," Satin smiled, leaving faster than he came in.

"Did you see that trick he did with his nose?"

"You are much too interested in other people's noses, my dear. Ever since yours was struck by that flying chocolate covered peanut. You should be interested in what that paper you signed without reading says." She sniffed before placing both hands on her hips.

Sweetooth opened his mouth.

"Don't you dare," the Queen ordered as she slipped a purple hankie from her purse and blew her nose.

The King shrugged and began to read. "This is a contract," he mumbled. His eyes moved slowly over the document causing his face to turn bright red, and moments later, flour pasty white

"What is wrong, Sweetie?" the Queen asked. "You look rather ill."

Sweetooth ignored her and read on, turning green at one point. Then blue. When he finished, he read it again.

"What is wrong?" Bonnie asked.

Sweetooth wouldn't answer, letting his head hang down until his nose practically scraped the floor.

"Look at me," she ordered.

Sweetooth hung his head even lower.

As she waited, the Queen wondered what could be so frightful on that tiny piece of paper. "May I read it myself?" she inquired.

The King could barely shake his head without banging his injured nose on the floor. "Yes."

Queen Bon Bon plucked the paper from the floor and began to read it out loud. "For helping King Sweetooth meet his candy orders on time, I, Sammy Satin, lay claim to his soul for all eternity and shall collect what is due on the day following Christmas. The signature below indicates the King agrees to the terms of this document."

Her eyes popped over the edge of the contract. "You signed it! Without even reading it! What were you thinking?"

The King couldn't answer. He sat on the bed looking like a lost child. He wondered how he could be so stupid and how he would ever get out of this hideous mess.

The Queen yelled out, "Ladies," and ladies appeared. Five of them, ladies-in-waiting, hovering over their queen who demanded, "Where have you been?"

"Waiting, my lady," they answered as one voice.

"Of course," she replied. "I need a bath." With that, she twirled around, being very athletic, and whirled out of the room. The ladies- in-waiting followed along, single file. "No talking," the Queen ordered as they left the room.

They didn't listen. They never did.

CHAPTER 4

THE ROYAL FAMILY ARE IN A BLUE FUNK

The King sat on his bed all day. He was in a blue funk, which was very disturbing because the Royal Family color was purple. Not blue!

The Queen was quite upset. "You can't even fall into a proper funk," she told him that afternoon. "Everyone knows our color is purple, not blue. What's wrong with you?"

She slammed the door on her way out and immediately fell into a blue funk herself.

Princess Candy Cane asked her why she was blue and the Queen told her, "because your father is, and a family that bears the same funky color together, stays together. I read that somewhere."

Princess Candy Cane immediately fell into a blue funk herself. She was a very loyal child. "There mother, feel better now?"

"Not really. Besides blue is definitely not your color."

Not yours either, the Princess thought as she mumbled, "Thank you."

"Shall we have a snack?" the Queen asked the Princess.

"Yes, but what kind of snack shall we snack on, Mother?"

The Queen was quick witted and answered straight away, "Blue Dolphin. That should be the proper food for people looking like us, Princess." Her eyes twinkled like twinkies. "Blue Dolphin!"

They skipped off toward the castle kitchen to find the cook.

"Should we be skipping around like this?" The Princess was out of breath.

"Nobody's watching, dear. I won't tell, if you don't." She snickered and skipped along so fast the Princess could barely keep up with her.

QUEEN AND PRINCESS IN A BLUE FUNK

CHAPTER 5
AGENT DOUBLE DOUBLE O O
TO THE RESCUE

That evening, Page came to the castle to see the king. A tall skinny fellow, wearing an I LOVE CHOCOLATE tee shirt and tennis shorts, was with him.

The King had finally managed to come out to the throne room and sat with his wife and daughter. All of them remained in a blue funk.

"Hi Candy."

"Hi, Page," the Princess answered, smiling so wide you could see all her teeth and some of her gums.

"Who is this man?" Sweetooth inquired.

All eyes fell upon the stranger.

"This is the famous Secret Agent Double Double O O, sire. He has come all the way from the Agent's Tennis Tournament in London, to see if he can help you with your problem.

"My problem?" The King pretended he didn't know what Page was talking about.

"Everybody in Candiesville knows, sire. That Sammy Satin is bragging about it every day at the factory. The other two as well. They are very organized and know how to get things done but nobody likes them. The workers are hoping for a miracle."

The King's face brightened for the first time in days. "They are?"

PAGE AND AGENT DOUBLE DOUBLE O O

"Of course they are. Even the people who aren't too crazy about you like Sammy and his henchman even less."

The Secret Agent stepped forward. "I feel I can be of service, sire. Let me see that contract you signed."

The King handed it over. "This is only a copy," he said. "Sammy has the original and we'll never get it back."

Agent Double Double O O smiled.

"We'll see about that." He turned and began to leave.

"What will you do?" King Sweetooth asked.

"That, sire, is a secret." He rushed off before anyone could ask him anything else.

"He's a creepy looking guy," the Queen told everyone. "Don't you think?"

"Maybe that's what we need," Sweetooth told her.

"Never judge a book by it's cover, father," the Princess added. "You always tell me that."

"Yes, I do. You have such a good memory, too."

Page stepped forward and spoke to the Princess. "Would you like to go outside and look at the stars?"

"The stars?" the King blustered.

"Oh, do be quiet, Sweetie," the Queen said. "Go ahead, my dear. Be careful of your neck."

CHAPTER 6

Secret Agent Double Double O O was the son of the famous Secret Agent Double Nothing, known throughout the entire world and in parts of outer space. It was only natural that little Oscar would grow up to be just like his father. Only more so.

In high school, he took advanced courses and graduated with honors. He was accepted at Harvard University in Cambridge, Massachusetts and earned a Masters Degree in Psychology. He took further training at the International School for Secret Agents.

He was very bright but odd. People never knew quite what to make of him, but he didn't care. He was twice as good as the other trainees. This is how he got his name. Instead of being

Agent Double O, O for Oscar, he chose Agent Double Double O O. He liked his choice even though it made the rest of his fellow trainees angry.

His father, retired from the Agency the year before, wrote Oscar a letter telling him not to worry. "You are a cut above everyone else and it is, after all, the work that counts. Always do your best," he advised.

This is the code young Oscar lived by and it had served him well. In three years he had become the most well known Secret Agent in the world. Page had read about him in the Sunday Candiesville Times, and called him to beg for his help.

"You don't need to beg," Agent had told Page. "It is my duty to help. I really hate how creatures like this Sammy Satin trick people. They have no sense of honor. This is what the world lacks today, Page. A sense of honor."

Page had been happy that Agent's attitude had been so good. There are still some nice people in this world he said to himself after he finished talking with Agent.

Now Agent was back in his room, at the Lollipop Motel, looking over the document Sweetooth had signed.

He took out his books on legal matters and studied all night. There was no loophole. The contract was as good as gold.

Agent took a short nap. Feeling refreshed, he came to the conclusion he would have to get the original document back from Sammy. That would not be easy. He needed a plan and a little bit of luck.

The plan he could work out but the luck was a different story. You can never count on luck. It either happens or it doesn't. "I will just have to work on this plan as hard as I can," he told Page the next day.

"That's all you can do. Your very best, sir. I believe in you and so does the Princess."

"How is the Princess today?" Agent asked.

"Not feeling well."

"What is the matter with her?"

Page sighed. "She has a sore neck."

"Looking at the stars can be a pain in the neck sometimes."

"It can be fun, too," Page said with a smile. "If you're with someone you like."

"How does Sweetooth feel about you liking the Princess?"

"He isn't pleased because I am not of royal blood. I'm just a commoner. The Queen is a different story. I feel she likes me and wants to see the Princess happy."

"So if I save him, he'll like you better because you brought me to him."

"That's what I thought, Agent."

Agent raised both eyebrows. "Ah!"

"What?" the Page asked.

"You brought me here so you could look good in Sweetooth's eyes."

"I brought you here to save the King and the Kingdom of Candiesville," Page pointed out. "Now if it helps me as well, what's wrong with that?"

"Not a thing, lad." Agent Double Double O O responded. "Not a thing. If I can solve this problem, everybody wins."

"*If* you can solve it?" Page cried. "You have to!"

"I'll try my very best. That's all I can do, Page. All anyone can do."

Page thought that over. "I suppose. But you must do your

very, very, *very* best! Please?"

Agent smiled, nodding his head ever so slightly. "Love has such power in our lives. Don't you agree, Page?"

But Page was busy looking at his feet with worried eyes.

CHAPTER 7

AN UNEXPECTED VISIT

The Peppermint Soda Shoppe was always busy on Friday nights. This Friday, everyone was there; Page shared a soda with Princess Candy Cane, King Sweetooth and Queen Bonnie sat munching peanuts in their special gold covered booth at the rear of The Shoppe, and Sammy Satin sat with his henchman, watching customers dance the night away. The dancers watched Sammy Satin back.

"You like dancing, boss?" Danny asked.

"With a pretty girl? Of course."

"Of course," Danny said.

"Of course," Billy repeated.

Of course, Agent Double Double O O must have thought, because moments later he entered The Shoppe and on his arm was a pretty girl. A very pretty girl named Desiree.

The Shoppe became as silent as an old time movie.

Blue, brown, hazel, green and black eyes followed Desiree as she sashayed over to Sammy, sitting with his friends.

His eyes, blacker than coal, swelled three times their

normal size as Desiree approached. When she stopped directly in front of his person, his eyes began rolling around in his head.

She smiled, showing perfectly straight, white teeth. "Would you like to dance, Sammy?" Desiree purred.

Danny and Billy fell off their seats.

Sammy was dumb struck, but not so dumb to refuse. She took his hand and led him to the area on the floor where all the dancers had stopped to watch.

Perspiration rolled from Sammy's brow into his eyes and onto his cheeks.

"That's strange," Page offered.

"What?" the Princess asked.

"Sammy sweating. Wouldn't you think he'd be used to the heat? Considering where he lives and all?"

Agent overheard this conversation as he joined the young couple. "Yes, Page, you would. But, as you can see, even the devil can fall into temptation."

"He'll never give up that rotten contract," Princess wailed. "No matter how far he falls. Never."

"One can never be sure of such things, Princess. Have faith."

"*You* have faith, Agent."

Out on the dance floor, Sammy stood struck with Desiree's charms.

"He looks like he's in heaven," Page noted.

"Not an especially good place for a person of his background to be in at the moment, is it?" Agent asked.

26

"No." Page smiled." And I'm just dying to see what happens next."

"You are, Page?" Princess Candy Cane's face took on a look of pure horror.

"That's just an expression, Princess," Page reassured her.

Agent Double Double O O leaned toward his friends and spoke with great calm. "Relax, my friends. Relax. This story isn't over yet. Not by a short shot."

The Princess and the Page stared at Agent in a most confusing way. "Short shot?" they whispered to themselves.

SAMMY SATIN AND DESIREE

CHAPTER 8

A TWIST OF FAITH

"Are you as good at sports as you are at dancing?" Desiree whispered into Sammy's elongated ear.

Sammy pulled his head back. "Sports?"

"Sports," Desiree pursed her lips as she said it and twirled Sammy around on the floor seven times.

Sammy looked woozy.

"Are you all right?" Desiree inquired. "You don't look very well."

"I feel just fine. Fit as Nero's fiddle." He tried to straighten up but Desiree grabbed him and spun him around again. "Stop! A minute."

"Why, Sammy sweetie?" She gazed into his black eyes with mock solemnity. "Maybe you're just not athletic."

"Of course I am! I'm good at everything."

"Everything?"

Sammy almost fainted when Desiree leaned forward and kissed his cheek. "Everything," he stammered.

"How about baseball?"

"The best."

"Tennis?"

"Even better."

"Basketball?" Desiree showed her white teeth in her most dazzling smile.

"That's my best sport," Sammy boasted. "Basketball."

Desiree looked around the room to make sure everyone was listening. They were.

"I challenge you to a game."

"You? A woman? Challenge the great Satin to a game?"

"One on one," Desiree answered quite seriously. "You, me and the basketball."

"You haven't a chance."

"I know," she agreed.

"O.K. What will we play for?"

"Pick something you want more than anything. Something you know you can't have. If you beat me, it's yours."

A slow evil smile spread over Sammy's face. The words flew out of his mouth. "I want you as my wife." He held his breath.

"*Me* as *your* wife?"

He jiggled his head in endless up and down motions to indicate yes.

"O.K."

"That's it?" Sammy asked.

"No. I want something, too. Just in case I beat you."

"Of course. Anything you want."

He thought the idea of a woman beating him was silly, and

turned to grin at Danny and Billy. They grinned back but there was confusion in their eyes.

Sammy didn't notice that Agent Double Double O O had moved to his side.

"Desiree spoke quietly. "I have everything I want in life but maybe I could help someone else out." She turned toward Agent. "What do you think?"

"It must be something important like your becoming Sammy's wife is important." He paused and acting as if the thought just struck him, he shouted. "The contract."

"What contract?" Desiree asked.

"My contract with Sammy," Sweetooth offered as he entered the small group. Everyone else remained quiet but slowly each one of them stood up.

"Your contract?" Sammy spoke to the King.

"Yes," said the Agent.

"Yes," Said the Queen.

"Yes," said the Princess.

But more importantly, "Yes," said Desiree. "The contract. I want the contract."

Danny and Billy slid up to Sammy and began tugging on his sleeves.

He ignored them and asked, "The contract if you win? You become my wife if I win?"

Desiree spoke, "Yes," quite clearly.

Sammy was in seventh heaven and didn't know it. He shouted to the twins, "She can never beat me. Never!"

"Have you ever played the game, boss," the twins asked in

one voice.

"Of course. When I was a child. and I was quite good at it. Like everything else I've ever done." He turned to Desiree. "When do we play?"

Agent stepped forward with a pen and paper. "Not until you sign this."

And so he did. With a flourish. "You will soon be my wife," he leered.

"Maybe yes. Maybe no. I have faith." Desiree remained calm.

"That's a terrible disease to have," Sammy told her. "Hideous."

CHAPTER 9

NO RECOUNTS NEEDED HERE

"At high noon," Sammy had demanded.

"High noon," Desiree had agreed.

"It will be very hot," Sweetooth advised.

Agent and Desiree answered. "We know."

Everyone left The Shoppe and went home for a good nights sleep.

The following day, the Royal Basketball Court was flooded with people wishing to watch the grand contest. Vendors sold hot dogs and cold drinks and provided candy for desert.

Sammy arrived late, dressed in black silk shorts and tee shirt with a logo that said The Devils.

Desiree was waiting in gray warm ups. She removed those to reveal red cotton shorts and a white tee shirt spelling out Candiesville across the front. Sweetooth had made them available.

"You're representing the home team," he smiled, "and we're honored as well as grateful."

The twins were allowed to referee. This worried almost

everyone in the tiny kingdom.

Desiree won the coin toss and took the ball out at half court.

Sammy winked at the twins and as he did Desiree pushed the ball through the air.

"What?" Sammy sputtered.

The ball swished through the net and Desiree took it out very quickly.

"Lucky shot," Sammy said.

"Really?" Desiree pumped twice and shot another perfect shot.

Sammy looked stunned.

"Lucky?" Desiree teased.

This time Sammy lunged at Desiree, hoping to foul her and get the ball. The twins would call it. Instead, Desiree stepped to the side as Sammy flew by and dribbled toward the basket for a short shot.

"Three zero," Desiree informed Sammy as he scrambled back too late.

"Do something," he insisted but the twins were helpless. Desiree never was touched. Nor did she need to touch Sammy or even come close to him. Before anyone knew it, Desiree had put a move on Sammy that left him flat on his face eating asphalt. She dribbled casually to the basket and made an awesome reverse dunk to win the game.

"And the contract," Desiree reminded Sammy after helping him to his feet.

"You cheated," Sammy accused her.

The residents of Candiesville moved forward, closing in on Sammy and the twins.

"I think that is an ungentlemanly thing to say to a woman, Sammy," Agent Double Double O O stated.

"How come she's so good?" Sammy demanded.

"She should be playing in the WNBA," the twins moaned.

"I am," Desiree answered taking the contract out of Sammy's hands and giving it over to Sweetooth. "Anybody want a recount?" she asked.

CHAPTER 10

ALL'S WELL THAT ENDS WELL

Charlie Chocolate Drop made an amazing recovery and helped finish up the last of the candy orders. Every single order was mailed in time.

Santa came to collect his candy and stayed that evening for the Candiesville Annual Christmas Candy Party.

Agent Double Double O O and Desiree stayed as well.

"I don't know how to thank you," the King told them during a quiet moment when everyone had their mouths stuffed with food.

"Don't be so hard on Page, sire. Remember, Sweetooth, he was the one responsible for bringing me here. Saving your life."

"He truly loves the Princess," Desiree reminded the King.

At this very moment, Page was sitting on Queen Bon Bon's stomach as she floated in the pool.

"Your wife certainly likes him well enough," Desiree said.

The King looked over and shook his head in agreement. "I'd have a hard time disagreeing with that."

"Yes, you would," the queen shouted back from the pool, causing the whole room to explode with laughter.

And so, as a wise man once said, "All's well that ends well."

And it is!

Printed in the United States
201294BV00002B/1-9/A